2.99

WITHDRAWN

.

My Pops Is Tops!

For Poppy Steve and Grandma G., my
children's grandparents—N.K.

For Andy—this Pops rocks!—J&W

GROSSET & DUNLAP
Published by the Penguin Group
Penguin Group (USA) Inc., 375 Hudson Street,
New York, New York 10014, U.S.A.
Penguin Group (Canada), 90 Eglinton Avenue East, Suite 700,
Toronto, Ontario, Canada M4P 2Y3
(a division of Pearson Penguin Canada Inc.)
Penguin Books Ltd, 80 Strand, London WC2R 0RL, England
Penguin Ireland, 25 St Stephen's Green, Dublin 2, Ireland
(a division of Penguin Books Ltd)
Penguin Group (Australia), 250 Camberwell Road, Camberwell,
Victoria 3124, Australia
(a division of Pearson Australia Group Pty Ltd)
Penguin Books India Pvt Ltd, 11 Community Centre, Panchsheel Park,
New Delhi - 110 017, India
Penguin Group (NZ), 67 Apollo Drive, Mairangi Bay, Auckland 1311,
New Zealand (a division of Pearson New Zealand Ltd.)
Penguin Books (South Africa) (Pty) Ltd, 24 Sturdee Avenue, Rosebank,
Johannesburg 2196, South Africa

Penguin Books Ltd, Registered Offices:
80 Strand, London WC2R 0RL, England

Library of Congress Control Number: 2006101755

ISBN 978-0-448-44441-3   10 9 8 7 6 5 4 3 2 1

KATIE KAZOO, SWITCHEROO

My Pops Is Tops!

by Nancy Krulik • illustrated by John & Wendy

Grosset & Dunlap

Chapter 1

"Whoa! Check out Mr. Guthrie!" George Brennan shouted.

Katie Carew swiveled around in her chair just in time to see her fourth-grade teacher running into the cafeteria. Her eyes opened wide with surprise.

Mr. G. was wearing a white sheet wrapped around him. A Christmas-type wreath was on his head, and he held a huge flashlight in one hand.

Just then a song began to blare through the cafeteria.

"Why is Mr. G. wearing a sheet?" Emma Weber wondered.

"Maybe it's supposed to be a toga, like they wore in ancient Greece," Jeremy Fox, one of Katie's best friends, told Emma. "And I know that music. It's from the Olympics."

"Your teacher is so weird," said Suzanne Lock, Katie's other best friend. "Ms. Sweet would never wear anything like that. *She* has style."

Mr. G. leaped on top of a cafeteria table and raised his flashlight even higher. When the music stopped, everyone grew quiet.

"I have come to announce the first annual Cherrydale Elementary School Family Olympics!" Mr. G. addressed the cafeteria in a loud voice. "Each class will be a different country. And this Sunday you and your parents will all be going for the gold!"

"What's he talking about?" George asked his best friend, Kevin Camilleri.

Kevin shrugged. "I think he just said we have to come to school on Sunday."

George frowned. "Oh, that's bad."

"The Olympics will take place on the back field. For every event you're in, you'll be teamed up with one of your parents. It's going to be lots of fun . . . and there will be food and prizes, too!" Mr. G. added.

George smiled. "Oh, that's *good*," he said, changing his mind.

"After recess, you will find out what country you are representing." Mr. G. smiled at the kids. "This is going to be a peaceful competition. Let the games begin!"

✕   ✕   ✕

"Ooh, I hope our class gets France," Suzanne said as she walked out to the school yard with some of the other girls. "That's my favorite country."

"Have you ever been there?" Miriam Chan asked her.

"Well, no," Suzanne admitted. "But I've read a lot about it. I know it's the fashion capital of the world. All the famous models work there."

Katie had been to France on vacation with her family. "The food is very good there, too," she told Suzanne.

Suzanne scowled. "But France is really known for fashion," she insisted.

Katie rolled her eyes. Suzanne sure hated it when someone knew more about something than she did.

"What does fashion have to do with the Olympics?" Mandy Banks asked Suzanne. "The Olympics is about sports. I hope they have soccer. Did I tell you guys that my team came in second in the county last year?"

"Only about a million times," Suzanne said.

Suddenly, Becky Stern took a running leap and did a flip in the air. "Maybe they'll have a gymnastics event," she said as she landed. "I'll definitely bring home the gold if they do."

Katie nodded. Becky was the best gymnast in the whole school. And Mandy was an awesome soccer player. They were both sure to do well on Sunday.

"Too bad modeling isn't a sport," Mandy told Suzanne.

Suzanne frowned but didn't say anything.

Katie knew exactly how Suzanne felt. Katie wasn't a great athlete, either. She and Suzanne were both on the school track team, but they weren't super-fast runners or anything. When it came to sports, they were just average.

"Suzanne, maybe you can make up cheers for your team," Katie suggested.

Right away Suzanne looked happier. "Yeah! Being a cheerleader is cooler, anyway. Better outfits."

Mandy turned to Katie. "Maybe you'll make a flag for our team to carry. You're so good at art."

Katie liked that idea.

"I bet we'll have to do lots of research on our countries, too," Becky said.

"We always have to learn stuff in this place," Suzanne groaned.

"Well, it *is* school," Katie reminded her.

Just then, Jeremy raced past the girls at top speed.

"He is so fast," Becky gushed. "He's the best runner in the whole fourth grade."

Katie choked back a laugh. Becky had *such* a big crush on Jeremy.

"I'm glad he's in our class," Suzanne said. "He's going to win a lot of medals."

"We have good athletes in our class, too," Mandy reminded her.

"Yeah," Suzanne admitted. "But Jeremy's the best. And we have Becky, too."

Becky smiled. "Thank you, Suzanne," she said, surprised.

Katie was surprised, too. Suzanne hardly ever gave anyone compliments—except herself, of course.

"Your class doesn't stand a chance against ours," Suzanne told Mandy, Katie, and Emma.

"Wanna bet?" Mandy argued. "We're going to beat you guys, big time."

Suzanne's eyes got small and angry. "Don't be so sure," she warned.

Katie sighed. What was it Mr. G. had called the Olympics? A peaceful competition? It sure wasn't starting out that way.

Chapter 2

"*Konnichi wa,*" Mr. G. said, bowing to each of the kids in class 4A as they entered the classroom.

"Konnichi *what?*" Kadeem Carter asked.

"*Konnichi wa,*" Mr. G. repeated. "That's how we say hello here in Japan."

"Wow!" Katie exclaimed as she looked around the classroom. Paper lanterns hung from the ceiling. There was a bouquet of pink cherry-tree blossoms in a vase on the table. Japanese fans had been taped to the walls. Mr. G. must have spent all recess decorating.

She bowed to Mr. G. "*Konnichi wa,*" she said.

Mr. G. bowed back. "Very good, Katie."

"I like your bathrobe," Emma Stavros told Mr. G.

"It's called a kimono," Mr. G. explained. "It's a traditional Japanese costume."

"So we're Japan in the Olympics, huh?" Andy Epstein asked Mr. G.

"Good guess," Mr. G. replied with a grin. He pointed to a white flag with a big red circle in the center of it. "That's our flag," he said. "The Japanese flag."

Mr. G. walked over to the corner of the room, where there were some pink paper flowers, miniature paper swans and lanterns, and small Japanese fans. "Those are for decorating your beanbags," he told the kids.

"Cool!" George shouted out.

Katie had to agree.

The kids in Mr. G.'s class didn't sit at desks. They sat in beanbag chairs instead. Mr. G. believed that kids learned better when they were comfortable.

Every time class 4A started a new unit, the kids got to decorate their beanbag chairs. When they were learning about birds, they used twigs to turn their beanbags into nests. When they were studying bugs, they covered their beanbags in tiny plastic insects and spiders.

"When you're finished, we'll have a traditional Japanese snack," Mr. G. told the class.

"Oh, yum! Are we having sushi?" Mandy asked.

"What's that?" Kevin asked.

"It's raw fish and cold rice wrapped in seaweed," Mandy explained.

"Ugh," George exclaimed, pretending to gag. "Gross."

"Blech!" Kevin added.

"It's delicious," Mandy insisted. "I eat it all the time."

Katie frowned. She hoped sushi wasn't the snack. And not just because it sounded awful. Katie was a vegetarian. She refused to eat anything that had a face. And fish had faces. *Fish* faces—but faces just the same.

"No, we're not going to be eating sushi," Mr. G. told the class.

Phew. Katie breathed a sigh of relief.

"We're having green tea cakes," the teacher continued.

"Green cake?" Emma W. asked. "I've never had anything like that."

"You will today," Mr. G. told her. "And I bet you love it!"

× × ×

"I thought those cakes were really yummy," George said as he, Kevin, Katie, and Emma W. left school together at the end of the day.

"We could tell," Emma replied, laughing. "You ate five of them."

George shrugged. "I hate wasting food. And there were a lot left."

"They were pretty good," Katie said. "But I still like my mom's cookies better."

"Your mom does make amazing cookies,"

George agreed.

"Wait up!" Suzanne shouted. Ms. Sweet had just dismissed class 4B. Suzanne, Jeremy, and Becky caught up with Katie and her friends.

"What country did you guys get?" Jeremy asked Katie.

"Japan," Katie told him. "It's pretty cool. You should see what Mr. G. did to our classroom."

"What country is your class?" Kevin asked Jeremy.

"Liechtenstein," Jeremy said.

"Lickin' *where*?" George asked.

"Liechtenstein," Jeremy repeated.

"I already know how to spell it," Suzanne announced. "L-I-E—"

Becky cut her off. "It's a little country between Austria and Switzerland."

"*Real* little," Jeremy said. "The whole country is smaller than Washington, D.C."

"Oh, man, that's rotten," George said.

"What is?" Jeremy asked.

"That you guys got such a weird, tiny country," George told him.

"It's not weird," Suzanne insisted. "I think it's wonderful. We got a *fascinating* country. Liechtenstein is very cool."

"I thought you wanted France," Katie said.

"Liechtenstein is even cooler," Suzanne replied. "It's famous for its skiing. And you know what a great skier I am."

Katie frowned. Actually, the last time she and Suzanne went skiing, Suzanne spent most of her time falling. But Katie didn't bring that up. She figured that deep down, Suzanne was kind of bummed about being stuck with a country no one had ever heard of.

"There's nothing new to learn about Japan," Suzanne continued. "Everyone's been to a Japanese restaurant. But who's ever tried food from Liechtenstein?"

"What is their food like?" Emma asked.

"I don't know yet, but I'm sure it's delicious," Suzanne told her.

"We had green tea cakes for snack today," Katie pointed out.

"Were they good?" Becky asked.

"So-so," Katie said.

"Big deal, green tea cake," Suzanne said. "Frankly, I think you're secretly jealous. I bet you all wish you got Liechtenstein as your country instead!"

Katie's eyes opened wide. "We do not wish that at all!" she exclaimed angrily. "We don't wish anything!"

"Whoa, Katie Kazoo, chill out," Kevin said, calling her by her nickname. "It's no big deal. It's just some dumb school Olympics."

Katie blushed. She was embarrassed for having shouted like that. But she was really upset. Not about having Japan for a country instead of Liechtenstein, though. Katie was upset because Suzanne had accused her of wishing.

Katie never wished for anything anymore. *Ever.*

Chapter 3

It had all started one horrible day back in third grade. Because of Katie, her team had lost the football game. Then she'd splashed mud all over her favorite jeans. But the worst thing was when Katie let out the loudest burp of her life—right in front of the whole class.

That night, Katie made a wish that she could be anyone but herself. There must have been a shooting star overhead right at that moment, because the very next day the magic wind came.

The magic wind was a really powerful tornado that blew only around Katie. It was so strong, it could blow her right out of her body

. . . and into someone else's!

The first time the magic wind blew, it
turned Katie into Speedy the hamster, the pet
in her third-grade class. Katie spent the whole
morning going round and round on a hamster
wheel and chewing on Speedy's wooden chew
sticks. Boring! When she'd finally escaped, she
wound up inside George's smelly sneaker. That
had been really gross!

And then there was the time Katie had
turned into Suzanne just as she was about to
go onstage for a big fashion show. Somehow
Katie had managed to put Suzanne's leather
pants on backward. And she'd had a really
tough time walking in those high-heeled
shoes. In fact, she'd fallen right on her face!
Afterward, Suzanne was really embarrassed—
and confused. She had no idea that it hadn't
really been her up there on the runway.

Then there was the terrible time the magic
wind switcherooed Katie into Jeremy's kitten,
Lucky. Katie felt just awful about getting into

a fight with her own cocker spaniel, Pepper. Pepper chased her right up a tree! Katie didn't blame him, though. After all, cats and dogs just don't get along.

The magic wind was the reason Katie didn't trust wishes anymore. And she was never—*ever*—going to make one again.

"I have to get going," Katie said, in an effort to get out of there before her friends asked any more questions. "Or I'll be late for my cooking class."

"I'm off to my modeling class," Suzanne said. "I want to work on my posture. I'm going to be standing up tall when Liechtenstein leads the victory parade!"

Chapter 4

"Mmm . . . tofu teriyaki," Mr. Carew remarked as he sat down at the dinner table that night. "This is something different."

"It was Katie's idea," Mrs. Carew told him. "They're studying Japan in school."

"We're not just studying Japan—we *are* Japan," Katie corrected her mother. "At least in the school Olympics."

"Oh, you're having the Olympics at school," Katie's dad said, piling some rice onto his plate. "That should be fun for you."

"For all of us," Katie told him. "It's a parent-student competition. Mr. G. says we're going to have a three-legged race, a wheelbarrow race, a relay race, and a sack race. I think there's going to be an egg-toss contest, too. And the whole thing starts with a parade of countries, just like the real Olympics do."

"Well, count me in," Mr. Carew said. "I love stuff like that."

"Me too," Katie's mom assured her. "I'm still a pretty fast runner."

"*Aruff!*" Pepper barked.

Katie giggled. "Sorry, Pep," she said, patting the chocolate-and-white cocker spaniel on the head. "This is just for humans." She turned to her parents. "The games start at nine Sunday morning. But I was thinking we should get there early to warm up."

Mr. and Mrs. Carew stopped eating for a moment and looked at each other. Katie gulped. She'd seen them do that before. It never meant good news.

"*This* Sunday?" Katie's dad asked slowly.

"I know that doesn't give you much time to get in shape," Katie said. "So maybe you should do some jumping jacks and sit-ups after dinner."

"That's not the problem," her father said.

"There's a problem?" Katie asked.

"This is the weekend Dad and I are going to Cousin Alice's wedding, remember?" her mother reminded Katie. "You and Pepper are staying with Pops."

"That's *this* weekend?" Katie asked.

Katie's mom nodded.

"But you *can't* go away this weekend," Katie insisted.

"You were looking forward to spending time with Pops," Mrs. Carew said. "You always have fun there."

"That's not the point." Katie loved her grandfather. "I can't miss the Olympics!"

"You won't have to," her dad assured her. "Pops's place isn't that far away. He'll drive you to school on Sunday and be your partner."

"Pops?" Katie asked, her voice scaling up nervously. "Are you kidding?"

"Why not?" Katie's mom asked.

"He's too old," Katie blurted.

Katie's mom and dad started laughing.

"He's not that old," Katie's dad told her. "And he's in better shape than I am. I think he can keep up with a bunch of fourth-graders."

"But everyone else will have their parents there," Katie said. "Can't you ask Cousin Alice to postpone her wedding?"

Katie's mom shook her head. "Sorry, Kit-

Kat. You can either be in the Olympics with Pops as your partner or not take part at all."

Katie sighed. That wasn't much of a choice. "I'll go to the Olympics with Pops," she said slowly.

"Good. That's settled," Mrs. Carew said cheerfully. "Now let's eat our delicious Japanese meal."

Katie frowned at her plate of teriyaki. Suddenly she wasn't all that hungry. How did you say, "This is *so* not good," in Japanese?

Chapter 5

"Wow! Check this place out!" Kevin said as class 4A filed into the school cafeteria at lunchtime.

"This is really cool," Katie agreed, looking up at all the flags on the cafeteria walls. "There we are," she said, pointing to the Japanese flag on the far wall.

As class 4A got into the lunch line, they made a point of walking right past the silverware tray. The kids in Katie's class didn't need any forks or knives today. Mr. G. had given them all chopsticks so they could eat the way people in Japan traditionally did.

"I just hope it's not soup for lunch,"

Kadeem said. "How would we eat that with chopsticks?"

"I think it's spaghetti," Emma W. told him.

"Okay, I can handle that," Kadeem replied.

After getting her spaghetti and milk, Katie followed her friends over to where the fourth-graders sat. As she walked over, she noticed Suzanne standing by one of the tables. Considering the outfit she was wearing, Katie would have had trouble missing her!

"What's Suzanne wearing now?" George asked out loud.

Instead of jeans and a shirt, like most of the girls were wearing, Suzanne was dressed in a red jumper-style dress. There were little yellow flowers embroidered over the bib of the jumper. They matched the flowers that had been sewn onto the apron that was tied around her waist.

"That's, um, some outfit," Emma Stavros told her.

"It's the official folk costume of

Liechtenstein," Suzanne said. "My mother bought the dress for me yesterday, and she sewed on the embroidered flowers last night. It took her hours."

"Don't you think you're taking this whole Olympics thing a little too far?" Katie asked.

"No more than you guys are," Suzanne said, watching as Katie struggled with her chopsticks.

Katie squeezed the wooden chopsticks tight around a few strands of spaghetti. Slowly she brought the sticks up toward her face, opened her mouth wide, and then . . . *dropped the spaghetti right in her lap.*

"Yuck!" she groaned. "Now there's tomato sauce all over my pants."

"Oh, forget these chopsticks," George shouted with frustration. He reached his hands into his bowl, pulled up a handful of spaghetti, and shoved it into his mouth.

"Real nice, George," Suzanne said, making a face.

"Thank you." George smiled, grabbing another fistful of food.

"Anyway . . ." Suzanne said, bringing everyone's attention back to her. "Liechtenstein is a fascinating country. They have their own soccer team, only they call it 'football' over there. They don't have an airport, though. You have to fly into Switzerland to get there."

"Liechtenstein is also the number-one manufacturer of false teeth in the whole world," Jeremy added.

Kevin started to laugh. "You're kidding, right?" he asked.

Jeremy shook his head. "No. That's really what they're known for. Skiing and false teeth."

Katie giggled. That sounded really funny.

Everyone else seemed to think so, too. Soon they were all hysterical. George laughed so hard, he fell off his chair.

"Cut it out, you guys," Suzanne insisted. "False teeth are very important! Especially to people who don't have any real teeth."

"They probably have vampires in Liechtenstein, too," George told her.

"Why would you say that?" Suzanne asked him.

"Because vampires are a lot like false teeth," George joked. "They both come out at night!"

That made everyone laugh even harder. Everyone but Suzanne, that is. She folded her arms across her chest angrily. "We'll see who's laughing on Sunday, George," she told him.

"You don't scare me, Suzanne," George replied. "My dad's going to be my partner in the egg toss and the wheelbarrow race. He's in really good shape. He used to be in the army."

"Yeah, well, my mother's going to do the sack race with me," Jeremy said. "She was on her high-school track team."

"I'm not sure which of my parents is going to compete with me," Miriam Chan said. "So I'm making both of them go jogging tonight."

"Who's your partner?" Emma W. asked Katie.

Katie sighed. "My grandfather," she said quietly.

"Man, that stinks," George said. "An old guy? Can he even run?"

"Yeah. I want our class to win the Olympics," Kevin said.

Katie knew that she should stand up for Pops. She should tell everyone what a great guy he was. And how nice it was for him to drive her back home on Sunday morning just so she could be at the Olympics.

But Katie didn't say any of that. She just sat there, frowning and staring at her plate of spaghetti and the big tomato stain on her pants. Somehow, not saying anything made her feel even worse about everything.

Chapter 6

"Whoa! Awesome!" Kadeem shouted as he slipped the white T-shirt with the red circle on it over his head. It was Friday afternoon, and the kids in class 4A were getting very excited. They couldn't wait for Sunday's Olympics.

"Japanese flag T-shirts!" Kevin exclaimed. "Thanks, Mr. G."

"Arigato," Katie said proudly as she took her shirt from the pile.

"Excellent, Katie," Mr. G. complimented her.

"What'd you say, Katie Kazoo?" George asked her.

"Arigato is 'thank you' in Japanese," Katie

told him. "I've been looking up Japanese words on the computer."

"Arigato," Emma W. repeated as Mr. G. handed her a shirt.

"You're welcome, Emma," Mr. G. said. He smiled at his class. "So, dudes, be sure you get plenty of sleep on Saturday night. And eat a good breakfast beforehand. Make sure your parents do, too. You're going to need all the energy you can get."

Katie frowned slightly. Somehow she thought Pops needed more than a good night's sleep and a big breakfast.

Just then the bell rang.

"See you all Sunday!" Mr. G. shouted as the kids gathered their backpacks and raced out of the classroom. "Don't forget to wear your T-shirts."

"Sayonara," Katie said to her teacher as she left the classroom.

"Good-bye to you, too," Mr. G. replied.

Pepper began to bark excitedly the minute Katie's dad drove through the gates of Pops's neighborhood later that afternoon.

"You know we're going to Pops's," Katie said, stroking his soft brown-and-white fur. "You're such a smart dog."

"And loud, too." Mrs. Carew laughed. "He's barking right in my ear."

"Pepper, down!" Katie ordered, pulling her cocker spaniel onto her lap.

Katie giggled when she saw the big sign on the gate. In gold letters, it said Marsh Manor. But when Katie was little, she couldn't say "Marsh Manor" very well. She called it "Marshmallow." Sometimes she still did.

All the people who lived in Marshmallow were grandparents, just like Pops. Most of them didn't work anymore. So the community was more like camp. Besides all the houses on the tree-lined streets, there were also tennis courts, a golf course, and a swimming pool. But best of all was the clubhouse. It was a big white brick building. Inside it had a restaurant, a gym, and a game room. Pops and his friends played cards and board games, as well as Ping-Pong and pool.

"Okay, we're here," Katie's dad said as he pulled up in front of the small white house.

"Ruff! Ruff!" Pepper barked loudly as he jumped at the car door. Katie laughed and opened it for him. Pepper ran up the front porch steps.

"I thought I heard my four-legged grandson," Pops said, opening the door. "Whoa! Nice to see you, too," he added as Pepper leaped up and licked his hand.

"Hi, Dad," Katie's father said, giving Pops a hug before he even put down Katie's suitcase.

"Hi, Davy," Pops said.

Katie giggled. Most people called her father David or Dave. But her grandfather always called him Davy. It made him sound like a little kid.

It was really hard for Katie to imagine her father as a kid. Every time she tried, all she could picture was a baby's tiny body with her dad's big grown-up head on top. It was *not* a pretty picture.

"Hi, Wendy," Pops greeted Katie's mom. "Are you all ready for the big wedding?"

"I hope so," Katie's mom said. "I packed in a hurry."

"And speaking of hurrying . . ." Katie's

father said, looking at his watch. "We can't hang around. Otherwise we'll hit traffic going to the airport."

"You go ahead," Pops told him. "And don't worry about a thing. Katie, Pepper, and I are going to have a great time this weekend."

"Thanks for Sunday, Dad," Katie's father said.

"No problem," Pops assured him. "I'm finally making it to the Olympics. At my age!" He smiled at Katie.

Katie forced herself to smile back. She sure wished she was looking forward to it as much as Pops was.

Chapter 7

"That was delicious," Katie said that night as she ate the last forkful of her grandfather's special blueberry pancakes.

"You were an excellent helper," Pops told her. "I didn't know you were such a great chef."

"Well, I take cooking classes on Wednesdays," Katie explained. "And most Saturdays my friends and I meet at our house for cooking club." She looked down at her empty plate. "I love having breakfast for supper," she said.

"I don't think there should be any rules about when to eat pancakes," Pops agreed.

"Basically, I hate rules!"

Katie had once said the exact same thing. And when the magic wind came and turned Katie into her principal, she got rid of all the school rules. What a disaster that had been!

"Well, there have to be some rules," she told Pops.

"True," Pops said. "But I don't have to like 'em!"

Katie giggled. Her grandfather was the funniest man she knew.

"Why don't you and Pepper go set up the checkerboard in the guest room?" Pops told Katie. "I'll clean up out here and then join you."

"Okay," Katie said, getting out of her seat. "Come on, Pepper."

Pepper wagged his stubby brown tail and followed Katie into the spare room. He climbed up onto the chair beside her as she started to place the red and black checkers on the board.

While Katie waited for Pops, she noticed the leather-bound photo album on the nightstand. "Oh, cool," she said. The book was filled with black-and-white photos of when Pops was a young man. Ones Katie had never seen before. They were really funny.

There was Pops, sitting on top of a motorcycle. He was wearing a black leather jacket and boots. In another picture, Pops was in swim trunks at the beach. He was making muscles with both of his arms. Katie turned the page and spotted a picture of her grandfather wearing a crewneck white sweater with a big letter *T* on it. He was holding a girl in a short skirt high up in the air.

"Oh, that's from my cheerleading days," Pops said as he walked into the room and peered over her shoulder. "I thought you'd get a kick out of those pictures."

"Your what?"

"My cheerleading photo." He smiled. "I look pretty good, don't I?"

"You were a cheerleader?" Katie asked with surprise.

"Sure was," Pops said proudly.

"But . . . but . . . you're a boy!" Katie exclaimed.

"In college there are boy cheerleaders, too," Pops told her. He turned the page. "See, there I am with my megaphone, shouting to the crowd."

"You're teasing me," Katie said.

"No, I was a cheerleader. And I can prove it," Pops said. "Watch this." He raised his hands high above his head in a V shape. "V-I-C-T-O-R-Y is our battle cry. GO, TEAM!"

Katie watched in amazement as her grandfather leaped off the ground with his legs spread to either side and his arms straight up.

"Wow!" she exclaimed. "That was incredible. Can you teach me that?"

Pops rubbed his back and sat down for a minute. "Maybe later. But how about I show you a picture of your father at four years old,

43

all dressed up like a girl for Halloween?" Pops suggested, pulling out another photo album.

"My daddy dressed like a girl?" Katie asked excitedly. "Where? Where?"

Katie and her grandfather spent the rest of the night looking at old pictures. It was so much fun, Katie forgot all about the school Olympics. At least she did until Pops stood up and stretched.

"Guess these old bones need a rest." He groaned slightly. "That cheerleading jump really made my legs sore. Good night, honey."

Katie sighed. If one jump was too much work for Pops, how was he going to make it through a whole day of Olympic events?

× × ×

Slurp.

Katie awoke to a big, red, wet tongue splashing across her cheek. "Good morning, Pepper." She giggled, wiping the dog slobber from her face.

Pepper looked up at her and wagged his

tail. Then he used his teeth to pull her covers off.

"I guess you want to go out," Katie said, sitting up in bed. "Okay. Just give me a minute to get dressed and brush my teeth."

Pops was still sleeping. Katie could hear him snoring in his bed as she walked past his room to the bathroom.

"Shhh . . ." Katie warned Pepper. "Don't wake him."

Pepper wagged his stubby brown tail.

A few minutes later, Katie was dressed and ready. She picked up a tennis ball and walked toward the door. "Come on. We'll go play in the front yard," she said.

Pepper jumped up excitedly.

As Katie stepped outside, she felt a cool breeze blowing on the back of her neck. "Whoa, it's chilly this morning," she told Pepper as they bounded down the steps.

But Pepper didn't seem to notice the wind. Maybe that was because it wasn't blowing on him. It wasn't blowing the trees, either.

In fact, the wind was just blowing on Katie.

Uh-oh. Katie gulped. This was no ordinary wind. This was the magic wind.

The magic wind grew stronger then, circling Katie. The tornado whipped around wildly. It was so powerful that Katie was sure it was going to blow her away.

And then it stopped. Just like that. The magic wind was gone. And so was Katie Kazoo.

She'd turned into someone else . . . switcheroo.

The question was, who?

Chapter 8

Before Katie could figure that out, Pepper started barking wildly. Katie looked out through her glasses to see two older men walking up the drive toward her.

Her glasses? Wait a minute. Katie didn't wear glasses.

"Hey, Max, what are you doing out in the yard in your pajamas?" asked the tall man with the gray ponytail at the back of his balding head.

Max? That was Pops's name.

Oh, no! Had Katie turned into her grandfather?

Katie looked down. Sure enough, she was

wearing Pops's red-and-white, polka-dot flannel pajamas.

Pajamas! *In public!* This was *so* embarrassing.

"Now quit playing with that dog and get dressed," the short man said. "We'll be in the clubhouse waiting for you."

"Waiting?" Katie asked. "For what?"

"Don't tell me you forgot about our Scrabble game?" the 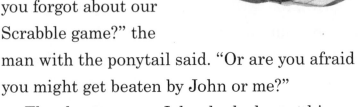 man with the ponytail said. "Or are you afraid you might get beaten by John or me?"

The shorter man, John, looked up at his tall, skinny friend. "You know what, Nate?" he asked him. "I think the champ is afraid to give up his title."

Wow! John had just called Pops the champ. Katie was seriously impressed.

She was also seriously awful at Scrabble. In fact, Katie had only played the game once before, when she was home sick from school one day. She'd lost really badly to her mom.

Of course, that had been a year ago. Katie was a much better speller now. And she knew a lot more big vocabulary words. Mr. G. made the kids in class 4A do a lot of vocabulary work sheets. Still . . .

"Not today, fellas," Katie told Nate and John. "I'm kind of busy."

"What, are you *chicken*, Max?" Nate asked.

Chicken? How dare Nate call Pops chicken? Pops wasn't afraid of anything. And Katie wasn't about to let his friends think he was.

"Just give me five minutes to get ready," she said.

"Great!" John exclaimed. "We'll meet you at the clubhouse."

$$\times \quad \times \quad \times$$

The clubhouse was only a short walk away, but today it felt longer. One of Katie's legs was very sore. Probably from Pops's victory jump last night.

As she walked down the carpeted hallway to the game room, she glanced at her reflection in the mirror. *Ew!* She took a step closer and peered through her glasses. Was that hair growing on the tops of her ears? Yuck! How come she hadn't noticed that on Pops before?

"Hey, Max, come on! We don't have all day, you know," John said, waving Katie into the game room.

"Coming," Katie said.

"Take your seven letters," Nate told her. He and John had already set up the Scrabble board and trays on one of the card tables. "John's keeping score."

"Okay," Katie said. As she placed her letters in the tray, she frowned with frustration.

E F C J N P O

What was she supposed to do with those?

"I'm going first," John said. He laid down five letters going across. "HIVES," he said. "That's eleven points."

"Good one," Nate complimented him. Then he added AGUE below the V. "VAGUE." He picked up his pencil. "Double-word score. That's eighteen points for me. Your turn, Max."

Katie stared at the board. What could she do? Finally she came up with something. "PEA," she said, placing a P and an E in front of the A in VAGUE.

"You can't do that," Nate said. "Because then your H and P are together, and so are the I and E. HP isn't a word. Neither is IE."

"What's wrong with you, Max?" John asked Katie.

"I . . . um . . . I just wanted to see if you were paying attention," she said.

"Yeah, well, stop testing us and start playing," Nate told her.

Katie moved her P and E tiles farther down the board until she spelled the word PEE. "Pee . . . but a different kind." She giggled.

Nate and John looked at her strangely.

"What?" Katie asked them. "It's a real word. I know because Suzanne and I looked it up in the dictionary once."

"You and who did what?" John asked, surprised.

Oops. Katie had almost forgotten that she was supposed to be Pops. "I mean my granddaughter told me that she and her friend looked it up once. Kid stuff, you know?"

John and Nate nodded.

Phew. That was a close one.

"So PEE is your word, huh?" John asked. He sounded kind of disappointed.

"Yup," Katie said. "Why?"

"It's just so much shorter than your usual words," Nate said. "And it's worth only five points."

"Yeah, you're slipping, Max," John added.

Katie frowned. She hated the fact that she was losing the game for Pops. But there was nothing she could do. It was all the fault of the magic W-I-N-D.

Chapter 9

Katie looked down at the letters she had left to use. She, John, and Nate had been playing Scrabble for about an hour, and all she had was a Z and an E. The Z was worth ten points. But what could she do with it?

Katie frowned as she looked all around the board. Then suddenly her face brightened. "Got it!" she cheered. "And it's a double-word score!"

Nate looked from Katie to the board and back again. "L-O-Z-E?" he asked. "What's that?"

"LOSE," Katie told him.

"That's spelled with an S . . . L-O-S-E,"

John told her.

Katie blushed. She knew that. How could she have messed up an easy word like that?

"Well, if you can't do anything else, the game's over," Nate said. "Total them up, John."

"You scored eighty-five points total," John told Katie as he finished adding up her score.

"Must be some kind of record," Nate said.

"Yeah, a *losing* record!" John laughed.

Katie frowned. John and Nate were being really mean to her. Well, actually they were being mean to Pops, and that was worse. Especially because it was all Katie's fault.

Tears were forming in Katie's eyes. But imagine what Nate and John would say if they saw Pops cry! Katie couldn't let that happen. She took a deep breath and blinked away any tears.

"Well, I'd better go home," Katie told her grandfather's friends. She wanted to get away from that game room as fast as possible.

But as she passed by the pool table on the way to the door, an older man grabbed her by the arm. "Hey, Max," he said. "I need you."

Katie turned to him. "Why?" she asked him.

"I'm having so much trouble with my shots," the man replied. "I need some help."

"From me?"

Just then, a woman with blue-gray hair walked over to the table. "Of course from you. Who better for Patrick to learn from than Max Carew, pool champion of Marsh Manor?" She smiled at Katie and blinked. "I just *love* watching you shoot pool."

Katie blushed red. She couldn't believe it. This old lady acted like she had a crush on her. Yuck!

"Come on, Maxie," the woman said. "Show us what you've got."

Maxie? Ugh. Now Katie knew how Jeremy felt when Becky talked to him. It was awful.

But not nearly as awful as the idea of having to teach Patrick how to play pool. Katie was no pool champion.

Katie had seen her grandfather play pool before. He was really amazing at it. Sometimes he was able to get all the balls into the pockets of the pool table without giving anyone else a turn.

Once or twice Pops had tried to show Katie how to shoot pool. But the stick was so long. She hadn't been able to control it.

Still, Katie was taller now. And she had Pops's long arms. Maybe she could play pool. Especially if she remembered Pops's pointers, like lining up her right foot, her right arm, and her chin in the direction of where she wanted the ball to go. Or remembering to lift the knuckles of her left hand up off the table when she rested the stick on them.

By now, a whole crowd of people had gathered around the pool table. Nate and John were in the group. If she could just get a few balls in, maybe that would stop Nate and John from making fun of Pops.

"Okay, let me go get a pool stick," Katie said.

"Uh, Max?" Patrick said.

"What?" Katie answered.

"You mean a pool *cue*, don't you?" Patrick told her.

Oops. Oh, yeah. Katie kind of remembered her grandfather calling the stick a cue when he was teaching her.

"You knew what I meant," Katie said, going over and pulling a pool cue off the rack. She watched as Patrick rubbed some chalk on his cue. She did the same thing.

"Okay," Patrick said. "I'll set 'em up and you can break, Max."

"You want me to go first?" Katie asked nervously.

"That's what *break* usually means," Nate said sarcastically from his place in the crowd. Everyone began to laugh.

"I knew that," Katie told him. "I was just testing you—again."

Nate gave Katie a funny look, but he didn't say anything.

"Okay, here goes," Katie said. She bent over the table, just like she remembered Pops doing. Then she curled her fingers and rested the cue over her knuckles. She stared at the balls on the table and tried to concentrate.

But that wasn't easy. Two women were playing Ping-Pong in the same room. Every time Katie tried to focus on the pool table, all she could think about was the sound of the Ping-Pong ball hitting the table. *G-nip g-nop. G-nip g-nop.*

"Come on, Max, break already," John urged.

Katie sighed, pulled the stick back, and . . .

Bam! She jabbed the white cue ball way too hard. It went soaring off the table! When it landed, the ball kept rolling right toward the Ping-Pong table.

Oh, no!

One of the Ping-Pong players was taking a step backward with her paddle. She didn't see the pool ball coming toward her . . . until it was too late. "Whoa!" she cried as she tripped over the cue ball. The woman lost her footing and fell to the floor, right on her rear end.

Katie raced over to help her up.

"What is wrong with you?" the woman shouted up at Katie.

Katie gulped. This was *so* not good!

"Looks like you've lost your touch at pool, too, Max." Nate chuckled.

Katie couldn't take it anymore. She was so upset, she forgot she was supposed to be her grandfather. She just felt like a fourth-grade girl who was being made fun of. And so she

did what any fourth-grader would do in this situation.

"Stop being so mean to me!" she shouted. Then she ran out of the room and headed for home.

Chapter 10

Katie ran as fast as her grandfather's legs could carry her. When she reached the corner before his house, she stopped and bent down slightly to catch her breath. She rubbed the top of her thighs with her hands. They were kind of achy.

Poor Pops. When he got back into his own body, he was going to be pretty sore from all the running.

And that wasn't even the most horrible thing Katie had done to her grandfather today. She'd embarrassed Pops in front of his friends. She hadn't meant to. But Katie wasn't Pops. She wasn't good at the same things he was.

Katie and her friends had been wrong to think kids were better than grandparents when it came to competitions. There *were* things older people could beat kids at. Things like Scrabble and pool. Probably plenty of other things, too.

Just then, Katie felt a slight breeze on the back of her neck. The cool wind felt nice as it gently blew on her.

But then, suddenly, the breeze wasn't so gentle anymore. It was getting stronger and stronger. Now it was a powerful tornado. *A tornado that was swirling just around Katie.*

The magic wind was back!

Katie grabbed onto a nearby mailbox and held on tight, just to keep from being blown down the block. The magic wind blew and blew, harder and harder. It whirled and swirled, lifting Katie's legs right off the ground.

And then it stopped. Just like that. Katie was back.

So was Pops. And boy, was he confused!

"How did I get here?" he asked Katie, shaking his head and looking puzzled. "The last thing I remember, I was still in bed."

"You . . . um . . . you ran here from the clubhouse," Katie told him.

Pops rubbed his legs. "That explains why I'm stiff," he said. "But what was I doing in the clubhouse?"

"Playing Scrabble and pool," Katie said.

"That really happened?" Pops asked her. "I thought I was dreaming."

"It happened," Katie said with a frown.

"I did pretty badly, huh?" Pops asked her.

Before Katie could answer, Nate and John came walking up to them.

"There you are, Max," John said.

"You ran out of there so fast, we couldn't catch up," Nate added. "We didn't know you were a track star!"

"We were just joking with you, Max. We weren't being mean," John told him. "But what happened to you today?"

Pops sighed. "I'm not really sure," he said. "It's all kind of fuzzy."

"Anybody can have a bad day," Katie piped up. She frowned slightly. Pops had had a *really* bad day—all because of her.

But Katie had a great idea about how to change all that. "I bet if Pops went back to the clubhouse right now, he could beat both of you at anything!" she exclaimed with pride.

Pops smiled at Katie. "Have you fellas met my granddaughter?" he asked Nate and John.

"No," John said.

"I'm Katie," she told the men, holding out her hand.

"When did you get here?" Nate asked her.

"Last night," Katie said. "But I was . . . er . . . I was still sleeping when Pops went to play with you." Okay, so that was a lie. But she couldn't tell them what really happened, could she?

"Just as well you weren't there," Pops said. "It was pretty embarrassing."

"Let's go back now," Katie told him. "It's a rematch!"

×　　×　　×

"Seven ball in the corner pocket," Pops said as he leaned over the pool table and steadied his cue. With one smooth motion, he tapped the white ball. It rolled smoothly across the table and knocked the seven ball into the pocket in the corner of the table. "Now it's just the eight ball left," Pops told Nate and John.

Katie smiled proudly. Her grandfather had already won the first two games easily.

Plink. The white cue ball knocked the black eight ball into the pocket.

Make that *three* games!

"And that about does it," Pops said cheerfully. He smiled at Nate and John. "You want to play again? Or maybe try a game of Scrabble?"

John shook his head. "That's okay, Max. A man can only take so many beatings in one day."

"I'll say," Nate agreed. "Obviously our Max is back!"

"He sure is!" Katie cheered. "And my Pops's tops!"

Chapter 11

"Okay, Katie, are you ready to win this three-legged race?" Pops asked Katie on Sunday morning.

Katie bent down and made sure her leg was tied tightly to Pops's. "You bet," she said.

"We're going to win it for Japan!" Pops agreed, pointing to his white T-shirt with the big red circle on it.

"On your marks, get set, go!" shouted Mr. Kane, the school principal.

And they were off! Katie was amazed at just how fast Pops could move when he got going. He was practically dragging her down the field. But it was working. Katie and Pops were in the lead.

Then Jeremy and his mother came up alongside them in their Liechtenstein shirts. They were moving really fast. Any minute now they would catch up to Katie and Pops!

"Come on, Pops, faster!" Katie cried out.

Pops picked up the pace.

But so did Mrs. Fox and Jeremy. They were neck and neck with Katie and Pops. Katie pushed harder. The finish line was in view now. Just a few more steps and . . .

Jeremy and his mom crossed the line just before Katie and Pops.

Pops stopped and caught his breath. Katie was breathing hard, too. She bent down and untied the scarf from their legs.

"Silver medal. Not bad," Pops said between heavy breaths.

Jeremy walked over and shook Katie's hand. "You almost won," he told her. "It was a good race."

"It sure was!" Pops said. "I can't wait for the next one."

"I've got to get a cup of water first," Katie said. "Do you want one, Pops?"

He nodded. "Thanks."

Katie walked over to the water cooler. Kids from all the grades were standing nearby.

"Wow, Katie, your grandfather's really fast," a sixth-grader named Selena said. The French flag was on her shirt.

"Seriously," agreed Evan, a fifth-grader in a shirt with the Spanish flag on the front. "My grandparents can't run like that."

"Your grandfather's cool," Selena told her. "I wish mine was here."

"Katie's grandfather *is* amazing," Suzanne said, stepping into the middle of the crowd. "Of course *I've* known him for years. That's because Katie and I are best friends. I like to come over to her house whenever her grandfather visits."

Katie rolled her eyes. Suzanne could always find something to brag about.

But Katie could understand why someone

might brag about knowing Pops. He was a really great guy. And an awesome athlete, too.

As Katie walked over to give her grandfather his cup of water, she thought about how glad she was that the magic wind had stayed away today. Right now she was really happy to be exactly who she was—Max Carew's granddaughter, Katie Kazoo.

Fun Facts
About the Olympics

1. The five Olympic rings are blue, yellow, black, green, and red. Those colors were chosen because at least one of them appears on every flag in the world.

2. The traditional lighting of the Olympic flame started in ancient Greece. Once the flame was lit, it was kept burning until the closing of the Olympic Games.

3. The ancient Olympic Games were held to honor the Greek god Zeus.

4. Olympic gold medals haven't been solid gold since 1912. Today the gold medals have a silver core and then are covered with a layer

of real gold.

5. In winter Olympics, Norway has won the most medals—263 in all as of 2006.

6. In summer Olympics, The United States has won the most medals—2,189 total as of 2007.

7. The official motto of the Olympics is "Swifter, higher, stronger."

8. Women were not allowed to compete in the Olympics until the 1900 Paris games. There have been women competitors in the games ever since.

9. The first modern Olympics were held in Athens, Greece, in 1896.

10. More than two hundred and three countries now compete in the Olympics.

About the Author

NANCY KRULIK is the author of more than 150 books for children and young adults, including three *New York Times* bestsellers. She lives in New York City with her husband, composer Daniel Burwasser, their children, Amanda and Ian, and Pepper, a chocolate and white spaniel mix. When she's not busy writing the *Katie Kazoo, Switcheroo* series, Nancy loves swimming, reading, and going to the movies.

$\times \quad \times \quad \times$

About the Illustrators

JOHN & WENDY'S art has been featured in other books for children, in magazines, on stationery, and on toys. When they are not drawing Katie and her friends, they like to paint, take photographs, travel, and play music in their rock 'n' roll band. They live and work in Brooklyn, New York.